The Magic Pea

PHASE 5

7b

Level 7 – Turquoise

Readers

Helpful Hints for Reading at Home

The graphemes (written letters) and phonemes (units of sound) used throughout this series are aligned with Letters and Sounds. This offers a consistent approach to learning whether reading at home or in the classroom. Books levelled as 'a' are an introduction to this band. Readers can advance to 'b' where graphemes are consolidated and further graphemes are introduced.

HERE IS A LIST OF ALTERNATIVE GRAPHEMES FOR THIS PHASE OF LEARNING. AN EXAMPLE OF THE PRONUNCIATION CAN BE FOUND IN BRACKETS.

Phase 5 Alternative Pronunciations of Graphemes			
a (hat, what)	e (bed, she)	i (fin, find)	o (hot, so)
u (but, unit)	c (cat, cent)	g (got, giant)	ow (cow, blow)
ie (tied, field)	ea (eat, bread)	er (farmer, herb)	ch (chin, school, chef)
y (yes, by, very)	ou (out, shoulder, could, you)		
o_e (home)	u_e (rule)		

HERE ARE SOME WORDS WHICH YOUR CHILD MAY FIND TRICKY.

Phase 5 Tricky Words			
oh	their	people	Mr
Mrs	looked	called	asked
could			

HERE ARE SOME WORDS THAT MIGHT NOT YET BE FULLY DECODABLE.

Challenge Words			
baby	cry	everywhere	

TOP TIPS FOR HELPING YOUR CHILD TO READ:

• Allow children time to break down unfamiliar words into units of sound and then encourage children to string these sounds together to create the word.

• Encourage your child to point out any focus phonics when they are used.

• Read through the book more than once to grow confidence.

• Ask simple questions about the text to assess understanding.

• Encourage children to use illustrations as prompts.

PHASE 5

76

This book is a 'b' level and is a turquoise level 7 book band.

She loved to read her mum's letters about all the animals she had helped. Being a vet sounded like the best job ever.

One day, Anya found something odd tucked away in her mum's bedroom. It was small and green and looked like a pea!

Anya picked it up. She saw that it wasn't just a normal pea. It was a magic pea!
"How exciting!" squealed Anya.

What did the magic pea do? Did the pea help Dad to clean the house so he can sit back and relax?

Did the magic pea help Anya to cheat and always win against Dad? Dad always beat Anya at chess.

The magic pea didn't help Dad clean or help Anya cheat. What the magic pea did do was help Anya to reach faraway places.

With the magic pea, Anya leaped around the world. She also spoke to animals to find out their problems. Perfect for someone who dreamed of being a vet!

Anya went to the beach and saw some seals. They were moving across the sand and looked sad.

"What is wrong?" asked Anya.
"Something awful has happened and we can't find our baby!" replied one of the seals, before she started to cry.

Anya followed the magic pea up and down the beach, until she found the lost seal playing on a seesaw with her friends!

"There you are!" said Anya. "What are you doing on this seesaw? Your mum and dad are looking for you!"

The baby seal went back to her mum and dad.
Anya waved and went into the sea to find
more animals to help.

Anya swam down to the bottom of the sea.
There were heaps of seashells everywhere.
Who was that behind the seashells?

"Hello," said Anya. "What's the matter?"
"My jaw!" cried the shark. "It hurts when I
eat, speak and yawn."

Anya rubbed the magic pea on the shark's jaw. All the pain went away! The shark was healed!

"Thank you!" smiled the shark.

Next, Anya travelled to a rainforest. She saw a macaw sitting high up in a tree. It was squawking and making such a loud noise!

"My beak hurts, and so do my claws," cried the macaw. "Please, can you help me?"

It was too hard to reach the macaw, so Anya threw the magic pea up into the air. It fell straight into the macaw's beak!

"I feel better, but I didn't mean to eat your magic pea," said the macaw.
"That's okay," sighed Anya. "I think I know my way back home."

It had been a long day for Anya. She may have lost the magic pea, but she had helped lots of animals first.

When Anya got back to her house, she saw that someone was waiting for her. It was her mum!

"Anya, you're famous!"
People knew all about how she had helped the seals and healed the shark and the macaw. But how?

Anya felt bad about stealing her mum's magic pea. And now it was lost forever.
"Mum, I need to tell you something," said Anya.

"You've done so well, Anya. You deserve a treat," said Anya's mum.
Then she got something out of her pocket.
"Look after this one," she said.

"Does that mean you took the photos?"
asked Anya.
Anya's mum smiled and they both yawned.
It had been a long day.

The Magic Pea

1. What job does Anya's mum do?

2. What was wrong with the seals at the beach?

    (a) They couldn't swim

    (b) They couldn't find their baby

    (c) They were hungry

3. How do you think it made Anya feel to help the different animals?

4. Who was waiting for Anya when she got home?

5. What do you think Anya's new magic pea will do? What would you like to use it for?

©2020 **BookLife Publishing Ltd.**
King's Lynn, Norfolk PE30 4LS

ISBN 978-1-83927-311-7

All rights reserved. Printed in Malaysia.
A catalogue record for this book is available
from the British Library.

The Magic Pea
Written by Madeline Tyler
Illustrated by Margherita Borin

An Introduction to BookLife Readers...

Our Readers have been specifically created in line with the London Institute of Education's approach to book banding and are phonetically decodable and ordered to support each phase of the Letters and Sounds document.

Each book has been created to provide the best possible reading and learning experience. Our aim is to share our love of books with children, providing both emerging readers and prolific page-turners with beautiful books that are guaranteed to provoke interest and learning, regardless of ability.

BOOK BAND GRADED using the Institute of Education's approach to levelling.

PHONETICALLY DECODABLE supporting each phase of Letters and Sounds.

EXERCISES AND QUESTIONS to offer reinforcement and to ascertain comprehension.

BEAUTIFULLY ILLUSTRATED to inspire and provoke engagement, providing a variety of styles for the reader to enjoy whilst reading through the series.

AUTHOR INSIGHT:
MADELINE TYLER

Native to Norfolk, England, Madeline Tyler's intelligence and professionalism can be felt in the 50-plus books that she has written for BookLife Publishing. A graduate of Queen Mary University of London with a 1st Class degree in Comparative Literature, she also received a University Volunteering Award for helping children to read at a local school.

When she was a child, Madeline enjoyed playing the violin, and she now relaxes through yoga and reading books!

PHASE 5
7b

This book is a 'b' level and is a turquoise level 7 book band.